In Daddy's Arms

A DDLG, ABDL story about a Daddy who can't believe he found a perfect little girl just like you

By Tina Moore

Table of Contents

Chapter 1

There was something about the way you looked at me that made me need to know your name. Was it your playful gaze or the sparkle in your eye, which told me that this girl was the one for me, I still don't know nor care. All I cared about was that after the first round of drinks when you suggested we head off to get ice-cream, I knew you liked me too.

"Hi honey, I'm home early. You won't believe the day I've had!" I called, placing my brown leather satchel on the hook beside the door. We moved into the large townhouse in the city years ago when I took a job with an international accounting firm. You loved the property the moment you saw it, telling me that we would paint a wall in the spare room pink and imagining where all your stuffies would go. It makes it even harder to tell you this, knowing how much you love this house.

I walk through to the living room and pour myself a drink to find you playing on the floor with the train tracks I bought you for Christmas. You are so engrossed that you don't see me sit on the couch and kick off my shoes. The sound startles you, and you turn around quickly to see me sitting there watching you.

"Daddy!" You gasp, making me chuckle.

"You scared me," you add, crawling over to me and coming to snuggle next to me. This is my favorite thing to come home to. I love the days that you have off because it means that you play all day and are really into your little space by the time I get home.

You pick up a train and run it over my head, messing up my hair and giggle when I playfully bite your toy and growl with it in my mouth.

"Daddy, give it back," you giggle before I give it back to you and watch as you settle back onto the floor. I sip my drink and watch as you play pushing the train around the tracks with my foot before I get up and go over to the kitchen bench and open my laptop.

"Is it alright if Daddy does a little bit of work before dinner, baby girl?" I ask as I pass you your sippy cup full of water. I have a feeling you have forgotten to have enough water today, and by the look of your grabby hands, you've just realized you forgot too.

"Yep Daddy," you say as you take a big sip and put your cup down just to pick it up again and take another sip.

"Ok, great. Just for a little while, and then I will make us dinner. I'm thinking nuggies and veggies tonight. What do you think?" I ask. You just nod your head as you wrestle with the tracks to make a bridge, and I turn around and begin working.

I feel a little tug on the calf of my trousers. I have been so busy with my work that when I check the time, I see it's already 7:30 and close my laptop lid.

"Daddy?" You also angrily question. I look

down and see your hungry little face looking back at me. I can always tell when you are hungry. You become a little monster!

"Ok little one, Daddy is done. I'll make dinner for you now," I said, picking you up and placing you on a chair. I pass you your coloring in book and crayons for you to enjoy while I make you dinner. I'm grateful that it'll be done in 15mins because by your grumpy little glares, I can tell you have a rumbling tummy.

"After dinner, we are going to have a bath and then get your work clothes ready for tomorrow, alright, sweetie?" I say, putting the veggies into the oven and the nuggets into the pan. You pull your lips to the side, and I know that you hate this idea.

"I can't have you being late for work like last week, baby girl. That's not ok," I say, reminding you that getting ready the night before is what helps make mornings run smoothly. Your pout turns into a smirk, and I flip the nuggets a few times to make sure they are golden brown. I can smell the veggies are almost done and open the dishwasher to find that it is empty. You have clearly done your chores for today, and I couldn't be more proud.

"Good girl," I say and watch your eyes light up, knowing exactly what I am talking about.
I plate up our dinner. I have cooked myself a piece of fish, nuggets aren't really my thing and set it down in front of you. You have started wanting to feed yourself dinner, so I give you your little fork but cut up your food for you. We talk about how your day was and what you got up too. I always love just letting you talk because you are so expressive and magical when you describe how your stuffies had to be separated because they were mean to each other or how you fixed your own problem when your crayons snapped.

"What about your day, Daddy?" You ask, reaching for your sippy cup. I pass it to you before placing my knife and fork down and sighing.

"Well. Actually, I think I should wait to tell you about my day until you're feeling a little bit bigger, baby girl," I say, laughing as I see you jump up from your seat and run into the bathroom.

When you come back fifteen minutes later, you have clearly showered and have washed your hair. You're wearing your red satin pyjama boxer shorts and a white racerback singlet, and I smile at you because you look so stunning.

"Ok, I'm ready," you say, your adult voice making me laugh. I must say, I love all the versions of you so much.

"I got made redundant today, baby," I say, watching as you take in the information.

"What?" You reply, making me just nod and shake my head. I had been with the company for the last five years and was really enjoying the job. But as the company merged with another company, my position became redundant.

"Well, that sucks," you say, standing up and going over to the bar to pour yourself a drink.

"You want another? I'll get you another," you say, making me sigh and smile at you. I love that you never pretend that a situation is good or bad; you just take it for what it is.

"What are your thoughts on what you want to do next?" You ask, coming back over to me and sitting on my lap. We silently drink as I think about your question. You pick at your food, using my fork, and finish your meal as I finish my drink.

"I think I will just take the rest of the month to think about it," I finally say, getting an agreeable head nod from you.

"We could always move. We could go somewhere completely different and start again by the beach or something. Get out of the city and enjoy a simpler life of surfing and morning coffee on the sand. Both take retail jobs or find work online?" You suggest. I look at you questioningly. I hadn't thought of any of these possibilities, and I see in your eyes that you are serious about your suggestions.

"Ok, well, give me time to think about it. I guess you're done being Daddy's baby girl for tonight?" I ask as you begin to grind on my lap.

"Yeah, I'm thinking Daddy needs his little

slut tonight. Come and let me fuck it all away, Daddy," you whisper in my ear, making me laugh. You always know just what to say, and I love it as I pull my cock out and pull your shorts to the side, pushing inside of you aggressively, making you take it as you sit on my lap. You wriggle, only adding to my enjoyment as I feel myself getting harder inside of you. It's not the most hard-core thing we have ever done, but it's what I need tonight, and I love that you give yourself to me so freely. I bounce you on my lap, feeling your tight muscles on my dick and hold you down onto me as I push into you, feeling you grind on me.

"That's what I needed," I moan as I feel my cock cumming inside of you. I don't even try to hold back tonight. I just want this release. You giggle as you try to keep me going, but I'm done, and with a loving slap on your thighs, you stand up and turn around to look at me.

"Well, now I need another shower, Daddy," you smirk. I watch as you slowly saunter away to the bathroom, cracking my neck and getting up slowly. I know tonight is just getting started.

Chapter 2

I decided to call in sick for the rest of the week. A little pettier than I would have liked to be, but I figured, if they don't want me, I'm not busting myself for them anymore. I'm glad I did. I was awake before you and watched as the sun slowly crept into the room and woke you up gently. The way you rolled around in the sheets before sleepily blinking your eyes open made my heart melt. There hadn't been a time I could remember when I had the joy of watching you wake up, and I am glad that this is something I am going to be able to do a few more times before I figure out what I am going to do with my working life.

"Daddy," you softly say, reaching out for me. I smile and pull you into my arms, brushing the hair out of your face and tucking it behind your ear. You rest your head on my chest, and I stroke your back, knowing how much you like this.

"What are you planning on doing, Daddy?" You ask. I just shrug my shoulders and softly laugh to myself. For the last five years, all I have done is suppress my passions in exchange for working long hours building someone else's dream.

"Maybe I look at different options. Maybe I could build all that furniture I have been wanted to build for all this time," I say, lost in my own thoughts about the woodwork. You sit up and look me dead in the eye. You have grown used to a very luxurious lifestyle, one which I am guessing being a furniture maker would not be able to maintain, and for the first time in all the time I have known you, I am afraid. Afraid that I wouldn't be able to give you what you want.

"That could be cool. We could go live in the mountains or something, and you could build your things and sell them, and I could find a local job doing whatever. This could be the thing that we have been looking for!" You reply, taking me by surprise. I love this about you, how you are always up for an adventure. We have been looking for something to spice up our relationship for a while. I guess the levels of comfort and routine had made things a bit predictable and mundane.

"I think you are right. I think we need a team-building exercise, and a change to the country might be what we both are looking for," I reply. We spend the rest of the day looking at real estate online in just about every semi-rural town of which we know the names. You've even got the maps online up to find ones we have never heard of, and we slowly compile a list of the locations that we want to research further.

"I thought you had work?" I say at nine o'clock, quickly jumping up and taking the breakfast plates away.

"I did. But I called in sick for this week too. I think this is more important what we are doing here. This is our life we are talking about after all," you reply, winking at me.

"From everything that I am seeing, I think we should just get land and build our own house," you call from the dining room table. I am still in the kitchen, trying to hide the fact that I am scoffing down chocolate. Before coming back over to you, I think about how that would work.

"We could finally have the house we have always talked about. With the nursery for you and the office for me. A library where we could store all of these books you insist on buying and an outdoor area that could have a huge deck and fire pit and hot tub. Baby, this could be amazing!" I exclaim, letting my mind get carried away.

"Aren't you glad I kept a tight lid on the money now?" You mock, making me roll my eyes. I know a lot of Daddy Doms feel that they are better equipped to handle things than their littles. I guess I used to be one of those guys too, but not after having met you. Some of my friends laugh when they find out my baby girl is the one who controls that money, especially because most of the money coming in is what I earn. But I have learned that it is better to work to the strengths of the relationship, and girl you are good with finances. I would be out buying lunches and coffees and all sorts of things on the daily before I met you. Not that we don't buy things we like, you have just taught me to be more conscious about what I am buying. I love that I have been able to learn how to budget and how to keep the cash flow coming in, and I guess that comes from understanding that we are a team. It's not me in control. It's us building a life together.

"Yes, thank you, little one. Daddy is very grateful. Because now I'm going to buy you a big house and fill it with everything you have ever wanted! Maybe me getting fired is actually the best thing that could have happened to us!" I say, picking you up and twirling you around in my arms.

"So does that mean I can buy that coffee machine I've had my eye on?" You say, a cheeky grin coming across your face.

"Yes. And it also means I'm getting that bed you've been finding excuses as to why we shouldn't get," I reply, doing a fake evil laugh and walking you over to the sofa before placing you down gently.

The rest of the day was spent by you doing very big girl things. You rang countless real estate agencies to discuss our situation that we were living in the city but wanted to move to the country, that we want land, and how much of it we are looking at and what attractions there were to the town. I was so proud of you as you crossed six out of the ten places on our list when they didn't seem right and narrowed our list to four places.

"I feel like we can handle looking at four places. Maybe we do one a week or one every two weeks, just seeing how we are going. Some of these are in other states sooo," you said, trailing off as you bite your bottom lip. I knew what you wanted, or moreover, what you needed by the look in your eyes and the way you were clearly done with working for the day. I chuckled to myself as I put the washing down and came over to where you had set up in the middle of the living room floor.

"Daddy's here," I said as I pull you into my arms and hold you tight. I slowly rock you back and forward and can feel you being in relax and unwind. Sometimes it takes you a while to shake off the day and let yourself be vulnerable, and I knew that today would be one of those days.

"Bubble bath and then dinner?" I suggest, feeling you nod against my chest. I stand up, grateful that my thighs are so muscular because from the tiny space I was sitting in, I was worried I might drop you for a minute. I carry you to the bathroom and expertly run you a bath. You reach for the bubble bath, and I let you pour it in, taking it away from you when you almost overdid it, making you giggle.

"Cheeky girl," I say, sticking my foot in to test the water. I gently lower you to the floor and begin to undress you, already planning on what I am going to redress you in tonight. I smile to myself, knowing how sweet and cute you will look as I lower you into the bathwater and watch as you lower yourself under the water. I hadn't planned on washing your hair tonight, but I guess you had. I watch as you play in the bath, pushing your duckies around and knocking them into each other, making missile sounds and getting water all over the bathroom floor.

"I think when we build our new house, we are going to need a bigger bathroom," I chuckle as water splashes onto my pants.

"Opps," you say, putting your hands over your mouth, seeing what you have done.

"I agree," you giggle as you pass me a towel and place it over my lap.

"Oh, thank you so much, baby girl," I playfully tease, knowing that the towel will do next to nothing. Some other guys I know would be so mad at your bath time antics or try to control them, but I can't do that. I like how free and fun you are, and if that means we get a little water on the water-proof bathroom floor, then so be it. I watch you lather yourself in Chanel shower gel and rinse off before reaching for me.

"Here you go, little monster," I say, placing

your monster hooded towel over your head. You snuggle into it and walk in the bedroom, instinctively laying down on the bed and playing with your bunny.

"Such a good girl," I say, talking out the powder, your diaper, and fluffy diaper cover. You sit up, resting on your elbows, and looking at me curiously.

"PJs?" You ask, tilting your head to the side. I love how you do this. It always looks so cute.

"Well, it's getting warmer now, baby girl, so Daddy thinks this will be better. Which shirt do you want?" I say, holding up two options for you. You look intensely at both choices before picking the light pink t-shirt.

"Good choice, baby girl," I say, coming back over to you and placing everything down. I take the diaper, and you lift your hips up.

"Thank you for helping," I say, powdering your body before fastening the tabs. I pull up the diaper cover and rub my hands over the material.

"So soft little one," I say before I take the t-shirt and pull it over your head. I stand back to look at you, loving the way you look and stick your paci into your mouth. You run your fingers through your hair a few times to help it dry. It's gotten so long you'll need to get it cut soon, and I make a mental note to take you to the hairdressers in the coming week. I know that we haven't had dinner yet, so I set you up with your toys back out in the living room and get to work in the kitchen.

I hear you happily playing as I make your pasta. Tonight I am making carbonara with a side of veggies. I am hoping that it doesn't take too long because I see you falling asleep, cuddling your bunny on the floor. I make a drink and stir the pasta as the house fills with the delicious smell and watch you lovingly.

I come over to you, your dinner in your little bowl, and lift you into my lap. You've been asleep for half an hour, and I've already had my dinner and stacked the dishwasher.

"Daddy?" You sleepily moan as you begin to

wake up. I smile down at you as I hold you, twirling the pasta onto the fork and feeding you.

"Oh yummy," you say, shifting in my lap, suddenly wide awake. Food has always done that to you. You could be in the middle of the deepest soundest sleep, but if you smell food or hear me in the kitchen, you wake up as though you've never even been asleep. I chuckle and hand you the fork, watching as you take big mouthfuls.

"Slow down, baby. It's not going anywhere. You don't want to give yourself a tummy ache, do you?" I ask, watching as you shake your head no.

After you have finished your dinner, I leave the dishes on the kitchen bench. I'll deal with those later. What is most important now is that you get into bed. I send you to the bathroom to brush your teeth and wait for you in the bedroom. I'll be so happy when you have a nursery all for yourself, as I am waiting for you; I imagine what it will look like and where all the new furniture will go. I want to make you a bookcase for all your books and a toy box so I can buy you more toys and have somewhere to put them. My thoughts are interrupted as you jump into bed and wrestle me onto my back, making me laugh.

"Oh, someone has a lot of energy now that you've had dinner, huh?" I tease, making you roll your eyes.

"Not that much," you reply, settling into my arms. I know that it will only be a matter of moments before you are falling asleep as I feel you are becoming heavy in my arms. I kiss your forehead and stroke your tummy, enjoying how your breathing slows, and your muscles relax as you fall asleep in Daddy's arms.

Chapter 3

"Daddy?" I hear you say in the morning. I sleepily look around to see that it is not only morning but late morning. I check my phone and raise my eyebrows. I must have fallen asleep when I put you to bed last night because when I wake up, I realize that I haven't moved positions all night.

"Hi baby, what is it?" I ask, rubbing my eyes. You bite your bottom lip, and I know what that means.

"Oh, it's alright little munchkin, Daddy will change you. I mean, we have to get ready for the day anyway. We have to do a few grown-up things today. Do you want to have your diaper on today?" I ask. Clearly, you have thought about this because you are nodding your head before I have even finished my sentence.

"Diaper on!" You exclaim squirming.

"But first, a fresh one?" I question, already

laying you down. I lay you down and begin to move around, getting you all clean and fresh. Once you are in a new diaper, you jump up and begin to look around for something you want to wear. You choose a pair of baggy jeans and a tight t-shirt, which makes your breasts look amazing. I shift uncomfortably, and you giggle, seeing that you have made me a little hard.

"I can't help it. You are just so beautiful," I say, kissing you on the tip of your nose. You wrap your arms around my neck and hug me tightly, so tightly that when I stand up and walk to the bathroom, you don't let go and I end up carrying you.

"Daddy has to get ready, baby. Can you go into the living room and tidy up your toys from last night?" I ask as you nod and begin to walk down the hall.

I strip off and throw my clothes in the wash basket before stepping into the shower and turning the water on. I let it run over my body and close my eyes before I begin washing myself. I think about the day, how we are going to be out for most of it, there is a piece of land three hours away which we are going to look at today and hopefully put an offer on. It's in my favorite location on the shortlist, and I hope you like it too. It'll be so great to get out of the city and find some quiet, peaceful spot to settle down. I can hear you talking to your toys, telling them that you will be back later and that you are going to go with Daddy to find a nice new place to live. You're so sweet how you do that, a few times you've actually had me thinking that the toys come to life the way you give them all such in-depth personalities.

I dry off and get dressed in a pair of jeans and a white t-shirt, not as tight as yours, but my biceps show off nicely. If I had any doubt, the smirk you give me when I appear in front of you in the living room would put my mind at ease.

"Oh, you like this, baby girl?" I tease, running my hands under my shirt and over my abs, showing off for you. You giggle and nod your head as I wink at you.

"Let's get breakfast on the way, I kind of want to get on the road," I say as I grab an ice-coffee from the fridge and a water bottle for you before getting my keys.

"Oh, ok. Hang on then," you reply, running into the bedroom to get your bag before reappearing.

"I really want this spot to be perfect. I want this one the most," you say as you walk toward the door.

"Same. If it is good, do we even bother looking at anything else?" I question. You take a sip of your water and shake your head no.

"Sweet," I reply and get into the car. I wait till you put your seat belt on before I turn the car on and head out onto the road.

You have spent the last hour singing to a playlist you created last week, and I had no idea you knew so many terrible songs. I laugh as you get really into them, grateful for the show because you and I have completely different tastes in music, and your performances make the songs somewhat bearable. We picked up bacon and egg rolls and kept following the signs which lead us into the forestry bushland, only stopping again when we finally got there.

Getting out of the car, we looked around and knew straight away.

"Ok, this is the spot," you say, taking the words right out of my mouth.

"Not too bad, is it?" I say more to myself than to you as we look around. The real estate guy turns up, and we exchange pleasantries before being told about the history of the land and what the attractions are in this town. To my amusement, the man seems very taken by you, and I catch him looking at your breasts multiple times. I won't mention it to you, though. I just enjoy that other people find you as attractive as I find you. We look over the property, and I am grateful it is a flat block of land. It'll make building the house a lot easier than if there were earthworks that would need to be completed. After twenty minutes, we leave your new admirer and head into town to see what the atmosphere is like.

Driving around the grid-like blocks, I place my hand on your thigh and feel your hand come on top of mine.

"It's nice here, hey Daddy," you say, playing with my fingers.

"Yeah, really peaceful. I'm glad we looked at this one. First, good call baby girl," I reply. It's a busy town of apparently just over 15,000 people. With the red brick, tree-lined streets and beautiful archways, it looks like something from a postcard.

"So, have we decided?" I say, pulling into a car space and getting out of the car. I thought it was best to eat something here before we drive back.

"Yep," you say happily, skipping over to where I am standing. I hold out my hand for you and enclose my fingers around yours as we walk down one of the streets lined with restaurants.

"What do you feel like?" I ask, looking at the street menu of an Indian restaurant.

"Honestly, I could really go a huge steak," you reply, taking me by surprise. I raise an eyebrow at you and chuckle as we walk to the steak house on the corner. I love that about you. Just when I think I have you figured out you switch the game up on me, you keep everything so interesting.

We walk inside, and both contently sigh as the air-conditioning hits us. A waitress takes us to a spot and hands us two menus. You'll have to read the menu yourself today because I have no idea what they serve here. Usually, when we have been to a restaurant a couple of times, you know exactly what you like, and I can order for you. I like doing that, but today that is not the case.

"I'll take the steak and mashed potatoes, please," you say to the waitress as she comes back to take our order.

"And I'll have the same actually. And two soda's," I add, knowing that you have great taste when it comes to ordering out. We sit in our window seat, watching the goings-on of the place we will soon call our home, and I reach out to take your hand, smiling at you.

"This is going to be so much fun. When we get home, I want us to find housing companies and start to have a look at the different options for us. I don't want this taking any longer than it needs to," I say, and you just nod your head and look into my eyes. Sometimes I wish I could read your mind, but I know that if you were unhappy, you would have told me by now, you have every other time.

We finish our meals and drive home, you've had a little nap in the car, and I have carried you back into the house and laid you down on the couch. As much as I wanted this to be something we did together, you are asleep with your thumb in your mouth as I search the internet for all the different types of house building companies. I don't mind buying off the plan, because I know that by the time you are finished decorating it, it will be transformed into something truly unique. I try to wake you, but you must be in a deep sleep, so I finish making a shortlist of the house designs I like and decided just to show you in the morning. I place a blanket over you and let your tired little body sleep on the couch for the night, whispering, "Good night, my beautiful girl," before kissing your forehead and going to bed.

Chapter 4

Silence. That is what I wake up to this morning. Silence has never been a good sign since you have come into my life. There can only be three reasons for silence. Either you are up to no good, you are making a surprise for me, or you have gone out for a run. I secretly hope that is it because you are making a surprise for me; I love your surprises.

"Baby girl?" I call, stretching and yawning before getting up. When no response comes, I get up and walk around the house looking for you that is until I see your note on the fridge.

Just out running, Daddy X

Well, that solved that mystery. I go over to the coffee machine and make an espresso and open my laptop, looking at the morning news. Usually, you are gone for an hour when you go for a run, so I know I have some time to kill before you get back. I go over the house plans, do some push-ups, and make a few adjustments to a playlist. Deciding that I need to wash the car, I take my shirt off, smirking at my muscular body, impressed with how I look and go out to the garage.

I get the hose, sponge, and detergent and begin preparing the mixture in a bucket. Just as I hose the car down, I see you turn the corner and make a break for home. I love that you always bolt home like a wild thing. Panting, you get to me as I begin cleaning the car, stopping when you reach me. You are doubled over, and sweat is pouring from your lithe body.

"Good run, sweetheart?" I say, picking up the hose and hosing down your body. You give me a thumbs up, unable to speak, and slowly lay down on the drive-way. I can tell you like it because you sprawl out like a starfish as your whole torso rapidly rises and falls. I make sure not to wet your face, but make your body glisten as your skimpy workout clothes cling to your body. I can feel myself getting hard, and I go back to washing the car.

"Yeah, it was good," you finally say, having gotten your breath back. You stay laying on the drive as I finish the car, hosing it down, and begin to dry it off. I take everything into the garage before coming back out to offer you a hand up. I can tell you went hard today because you are stiff walking back into the house.

"I hope you didn't overdo it, honey," I say, watching as you strip and throw your clothes straight into the washing machine.

"I don't think I did. I just really needed that," you reply, getting into the shower. You yawn, and I watch as you begin to roll your hips and dance for me slowly.

"Tease. Do you want breakfast?" I ask, getting up to walk away. I see you nod your head, and I walk out to get your muesli ready. When I first became a Daddy, I thought that it meant that I could just fuck my girl whenever I wanted. You quickly showed me that my ideas were very wrong. I remember when you used to tease me just to get me hard only to tell me that you didn't want to have sex, you just enjoyed teasing me. I had stupidly thought that was something only I was permitted to do. I had so much to learn, and I am so grateful that you taught me so patiently.

"Oh, thanks, Daddy," you say, breaking my train of thought. You are sitting up at the bench and begin to munch down on your breakfast before I can reply.

"What are we going to do today?" You say between mouthfuls. I honestly hadn't thought about what we would do. We have just been living in a strange little bubble of being able to do whatever we want whenever we want for a little over a month now as we wait for the house to be built. That should take roughly another six months. That means six more months of what feels like a massive holiday.

"Want to go to the zoo?" I suggest. I am actually running out of ideas on what we can do. We have gone to the aquarium, seen every movie that is screening, gone on picnics, climbed up mountains, gone to the beach multiple times, and even gone go-karting. You make a thoughtful face and then very enthusiastically nod your head.

"Cool, well, finish your breakfast, and then we can get ready to leave," I say, clapping my hands together. I must say I am pretty excited to take you. I can't wait to buy you a few animal stuffies.

We arrive at the zoo an hour later. You've got on your cute overalls and white t-shirt underneath. Pink low cut sneakers and a navy baseball cup and your beautiful blonde wavy hair flowing in the breeze. Sometimes I look at you, and your sparkly blue eyes and cheeky smile take my breath away, today is one of those days. You hold my hand, and we walk around the enclosures. You take about million photos of the animals, and almost as many selfies and photos of me. I love how happy you are seeing everything, and we stop to pick up two maps. I get the more in-depth map, and I get you a picture map, making you giggle. I love that you are my little girl in public, even though no one else would be able to realize it. We stop for lunch by a narrow river that runs through the entire zoo. It's beautiful with shady trees creating nice cool pockets to lounge underneath.

"Daddy, this is heaven," you whisper into my ear as you sit down and take a hot chip in your fingers. I have bought us hot chips and cold chicken sandwiches and sodas, and I watch as you put the chips onto the sandwich.

"You should try it!" You exclaim and take a big bite, clearly delighting in your choices. I just laugh and shake my head, lay down on the grass and look up at the clouds.

"How nice is this?" I say, stroking your thigh as you eat your lunch. I reach over to take a chip before taking a sip of soda. If I had known I was missing out on so much living, I would have made it my plan to resign years ago. I am sure I have added years onto my life by not being in that high-stress environment, and I really do believe that my aging has slowed down. I look over to you, staring intently at me.

"What are you thinking about?" You say, just before you finish your sandwich.

"That this is perfect. We are going to have such a nice life in our new home and new town. I think maybe we should consider moving there in a month or so and just rent while we settle in and find jobs? I just want to build my furniture and maybe work at a local store doing whatever. What do you think?" I say. I have obviously taken you by surprise as you choke on your soda.

"Um, yeah, ok. I mean, there's nothing we are doing here just hanging out and having fun. But I get what you mean, like as much as this is lovely, it might be smart to move and find new jobs. I want a job doing whatever as well. I honestly don't care what I do. I just want a simple, stress-free happy life," you reply. I smile at you and see you have had a cheeky idea.

"But before we go, I want to stockpile all the nice things from here that we can't get in our new home. Including all the zoo stuffies," you say, almost giggling. I roll my eyes, knowing that your list will cost a couple of thousand before tickling you and nodding my head. We finish lunch and go to the gift shop. You find an elephant, alligator, lion, and monkey stuffie, and I smile as I see how they are almost over-flowing from your arms.

"That's all you want?" I question raising an eyebrow. You nod your head and bite your bottom lip, looking around to see if you have missed anything.

"Yes, that's everything," you reply joyfully. I pick up a block of chocolate with animals on it, and head to the register.

"This one is Freckles, and this one is Sasha, and this one is Samera, and this is Cody," you say on the car ride home. I have listened to you for twenty minutes babbling to yourself about your animals, and I realize I must have been smiling the whole time because my face hurts.

"They are great names, baby girl," I reply, pulling into the driveway.

"When we get inside, it's bath time, and

then you can play until bedtime," I say, unbuckling your belt. You yawn, and I know that the minute I get you into your onesie for bed, you will be fighting to not fall asleep.

"Ok?" I prompt.

"We are home now, baby girl, I want to hear you say, Daddy," I remind you. It's not very often that I have to remind you of the rules.

"Ok, Daddy," you say sweetly. You place your new stuffies on the bed and then let me strip you naked. You didn't use your diaper today, and I know why. You hate being changed in public, but I raise my eyebrow at you.

"We are home now, little one, time to be a good girl," I say and feel you wet your diaper immediately.

"I bet that feels better," I say, feeling how full you made it. You nod, and I take it off you and put you straight into the bath.

"Daddy, why aren't we having dinner?" You ask as I wash all the zoo dirt off you. I wet your hair, and you point to which shampoo you want me to use.

"I already told you, princess. We ate before we left the zoo, and that would be dinner. You even had lunch at the zoo. You can't tell me that that little tummy of yours is still hungry?" I ask as I wash you clean. You think for a moment before answering.

"Maybe just for milkies," you reply, and I smile at you. I stand you up in the bath and rinse you off, making sure to hold you steady as you get out of the bath-tub. I place a towel down, and I hold you in my arms as I dry you. Picking you up, I take you into the bedroom, diaper and dress you and let you play in bed with your new toys as I go to make you a bottle.

I am gone for ten minutes and coming back into the room. I find you asleep, sucking on your paci and surrounded by your toys. You will be sleepy tomorrow as well, and I chuckle to myself as I place your bottle down and head into the bathroom for my own shower.

Chapter 5

I can tell that you have had enough of being a big girl for a day or so by how moody you are in the morning. It took me a moment, but I finally realized that it is probably because moving is big and somewhat scary.

"Are you nervous about moving, little one?" I say in a loving tone as I come over with pancakes.

"No," you pout, giving yourself away. I sit next to you and begin to take off your clothes, rolling my eyes as you make it as hard for me as you possibly can.

"I don't wanna," you fuss as I pick you and carry you to the bathroom. I ignore you as you thrash around in my arms, I don't take your behavior offensively when you are like this, and I know you are overstimulated and just need calming down. I run a bath and put you down into the water, watching as you grumble as you begin to throw your toys at the bathroom wall.

"That's enough. I know you are overwhelmed, but you still need to be a good girl for Daddy. I don't want to have to punish you, young lady," I warn, making you settle and being to breathe through the panic attack you are experiencing.

"There's my good girl. You're alright. Daddy is right here. If you don't want to move, we don't have to sweetheart, I am happy anywhere with you," I say, letting you cuddle onto my arm as your breathing remains at the quickened pace. I take the washcloth and begin to bathe you, seeing how your muscles start to relax, and your color comes back to your face.

"Daddy, I am sorry," you say in a little voice and begin to cry.

"You don't have to be sorry, honey. Daddy's got you. You're safe in Daddy's arms. Nothing bad is going to happen, baby girl," I soothingly say as I comfort you.

"It's not that I don't want to move, it's just

that it's big, you know, Daddy?" You finally say. I nod my head and look at you lovingly.

"Yeah, I know it's big. But you've got me, and you're going to love it there. You loved it there today, didn't you?" I ask, suddenly worried that you maybe didn't like it as much as I thought you did.

"I did. It's just that I guess it just sunk in now, and it sunk in all at once. But I want to move, I've already got my eye on the shop I want to work at, and I really want to build the house of our dreams," you say, beaming up at me. Confident that you have calmed down, I take you out of the bath and put you in a fresh diaper and onesie.

"But I thought you wanted to go over house plans?" You say confused when I zip you up.

"I do, but I think you need a little downtime. And that's what you are going to get," I reply, pushing a paci into your mouth and taking you into the living room and putting on some cartoons.

"I love you, Daddy," you say from behind you, paci.

"I love you too, baby girl," I reply, going over the house designs next to you. You steal little glances every now and then and point to the things you like. I think this is the best way to plan the house, giving you little peaks at it all.

****

The weeks seem to be flying past us now, and I feel as though I can hardly catch up. It has been really exciting, watching as the house takes shape, and you were so happy when we have been able to take photos of almost every major stage of development. I decided we should celebrate and have organized a play date with another little and her Daddy for you tonight. I know you'll be so excited because we have been doing a lot of grown-up stuff lately, especially this week, and you've hardly had any little time at all. I hate how life can sometimes demand so much from us that we can't have any downtime, that's what tonight is all about.

You come home at 5:30 to see that they have already arrived. Harmony and her Daddy Travis are in the living room, and we are all talking and relaxing when the door opens.

"Here she is," I say, jumping up and greeting you. You look around the living room questioningly, and I take your bag from your shoulder.

"We have been really under the pump lately, and I thought that maybe we should have a little downtime tonight. So I've invited Harmony and Travis over," I explain. I love that happy look on your face, and you go over to Harmony and hug her tightly, squealing with excitement.

"Hi Travis," you say when you finally let Harmony go.

"This is so nice, thank you, Daddy," you say, running down the hall with Harmony. Travis and I know exactly what you two are up to the minute we hear the hairdryer going.

"Hairdressers," we both say and lean back

on the couch to finish our beers. I have loved having Travis and Harmony in our lives. I feel that it is so important to reach out and not go into this kink alone especially for all those times where I have felt that I have let you down or felt bad for punishing you, it's been good to have Travis to bounce that all off. As we sit and talk, we hear giggles and gasps coming from the bathroom, and we have both learned that as long as there is noise, there is nothing to worry about. It's the silence that makes us concerned and nothing more concerning when there is silence, and then loud crying.

We rush over to where you two are to see that you have dropped the hairdryer on your foot. Harmony looks horrified, and you are grabbing your toes.

"Oh, sweetie, come here," I say, picking you up and rocking you in my arms.

"Did it land on your feeties?" I ask, seeing you bite your bottom lip. You nod your head, and I take you out into the living room, followed by Harmony and Travis. I sit you down on the couch and go over to the kitchen to get an ice pack from the freezer and wrap a cloth around it.

"Here, princess. Do you think some dino nuggies would make you feel better?" I ask, Harmony nods her head making you laugh.

"We can share them," you say, holding the ice pack to your toes. Harmony takes out her colors and paper from her bag and begins to draw a picture, I'm assuming for you, as Travis and I go to organize the snacks.

"Let's make it a rainbow drawing," you say to Harmony, who is busy color coordinating the crayons. You two have always had the sweetest friendship. On paper, you two would seem like the two most unlikely friends. You like everything to be your way, and she has the same desire; however, you both have always found a way to compromise. You take the pink crayon and move the remaining crayons in the line Harmony has made together, so there is no gap making you both giggle. I know that you are having a good time, and that makes me so happy. I never thought that someone else's happiness could make me feel this way. My heart feels so full and content when I see you are having a good time.

The night progresses, you and Harmony play tea parties and dress-ups, putting on a fashion parade for Travis and myself. At 9:30, I put on cartoons and turn the lights down, hoping that you begin to wind down for the evening. Travis and I give you and Harmony warm milk, I hold you in my arms and bottle feed you, knowing that it makes you even sleepier. By ten, Travis is walking Harmony to the car, and I am carrying you to bed.

"Goodnight, my beautiful girl," I whisper as I kiss your cheek and lay next to you. You roll over and snuggle into me, humming softly and happily as I tuck you in.

It's been a few days, and we have been busy tidying the house and culling some of your toys. You have made three piles. One is the yes pile of all the things you want to take to the new house, one is a maybe pile, and one is the donate pile. It's taken you three days to go through all your things, and it has crossed my mind more than once that perhaps I spoil you. Lucky for me, you've never turned into a brat, so I lose track of all the things I buy you, much to your delight.

"Daddy, are you going to go through your things soon?" You ask. At this stage, you are just sitting on the living room floor, throwing toys into the different piles. It's quite amusing to watch if I'm honest.

"Yeah, baby. But my stuff is easy to go through because I own like ten things," I only half-joke. I indeed buy you more things than I do myself, but it is because I don't really like having a heap of stuff. I'd rather have a few things that are really *me* and that way I don't have to make so many decisions, like what to wear, for instance.

"Daddy, you have more than ten things, you have eleven," you giggle. Cheeky girl, you are so wrapped up in your joke you fall backward, and now I am the one laughing.

Chapter 6

It's moving day, and we have ordered a large truck to take all our things to a storage facility in our new town. We have decided to rent a small apartment for six months while the house gets built and for us to get new jobs. The savings have started to run out, and I am nervous that if we don't get jobs within two months, we will be in dire straits.

The day feels like a blur. Everything gets packed into the car that we are taking to the apartment. Luckily I was able to find one which was fully furnished, so we only need our clothes, your little things, and our toiletries. Everything else is going into storage.

We drive the 3 hours to the town, help unload the truck at the storage facility, and then go on to the real estate to get the keys to our rental before moving our stuff inside. The next time I feel as though I can actually breathe is when we are both sitting on the couch, and I breathe a sigh of exhaustion and relief.

"I feel the same," you say. I look over at you, and you look, unlike anything I have ever seen you look like before. Your hair is a mess, your clothes are dirty and sweaty, and you have dirt on your cheek. Your little eyes are screaming with exhaustion, and I hear your tummy rumbling.

"Let's just order pizza and be done with it, baby girl. Can you shower yourself tonight? I don't think I have the energy to do anything more than stuff my face, shower, and crash in bed," I say. I feel bad for not being able to give you any real little time tonight for about a second before you speak.

"Yeah, I am not in the mode to be little right now anyway, so this works out well," you reply, making me sleepily laugh. You get up and drag your feet to the bathroom while I order the pizza and hope I don't fall asleep before it comes.

I didn't make it. The next time I open my eyes, you are eating pizza in the middle of the living room floor, watching cartoons in the middle of the night. I blink my eyes open to try and make sense of the scene I am seeing, and as I begin to piece together the parts, you look over at me and smile.

"Hey, Daddy. You fell asleep. Your pizza is in the oven, so it didn't get too cold," you say. I can smell a rank smell and realize to my horror it is me. I don't remember smelling this bad since I was in college, and I get up and go take a shower immediately.

When I come back, it is you who has fallen asleep. I guess having your tummy full of pizza is what tipped you into sleepy land. I smile and pick you up, carrying you to your new, temporary bed before going back to eat my now definitely cold pizza.

"So. The job hunting begins," you say over morning coffee. I look up from the newspaper and look at you. I can't believe that you are so beautiful and want me sometimes, today is one of those times. Whenever we go out, the attention is all on you, and I remember feeling so self-conscious when we first started dating because I thought something was on my face or maybe my hair was a mess. But it was you. They were looking at how beautiful you were.

"It does. There are a few positions advertised in the paper. Here," I say, folding the paper over and giving it to you. You scan over the availabilities and smile.

"Is it wrong that I think it will be really easy to get a new job? It doesn't seem that there is much competition. I mean, they haven't really even said what qualifications they are looking for. *Responsible and reliable* is hardy a difficult attribute to possess. Or I could be very mistaken, and we have move to a place where we truly are in a league of our own," you say, making me laugh. It has been a long time since either of us have been 'big fish in little ponds,' and I must admit, I am excited to get back to feeling superior to everyone else. I know it is a little bit of a bad excitement to have, but I've never lied to you about who I am.

"Ok. Let's make it a race. The first person to secure a job is the winner, obviously, but the winner gets to have a night of anything they want," you say, giving me the look of pure challenge, and there is no way that I am going to back down from this challenge. I know what I want, and I will be damned if I just give you the victory.

"Deal," I say, grabbing my wallet and heading toward the front door.

"Wait!" You exclaim, making me laugh and begin to run.

"Oh no, you want to throw down, baby girl, you're playing with the big dogs now!" I yell as a shut the door before you make it outside and begin to walk into town.

"You'll need all the head start you can get," you yell from the apartment. You'll need to get dressed before you can try and find a job, so I am quietly confident I've got this in the bag.
I walk into the few shops and make small talk with

the owners. This town is like something from a movie, with all the people who own the shops actually working there. There are no chain stores here, and that gives the town a lovely feel. After about half an hour of walking through town and talking to the people, I see you walk down the street and nearly walk into a family coming in the other direction.

"Hey, whoa, you look good," I say, looking around, trying not to get hard. You've decided to up the stakes I see as you are wearing your new black heels, black stockings, and black denim skirt. You've got a loose-fitting white satin blouse on, and your lips are painted a dark but muted shade of crimson. Your blonde hair is flowing elegantly in the wind, and I have a feeling that if that wasn't enough to do it, your black eyeliner will have you winning this throw down.

"Yeah, I know, baby," you say with a wink, pushing past me and going into a beauty salon. I wonder what you are planning to do there since you don't know the trade. I decide to wait for you, mostly because I can't take myself away from you and sit down on a street bench.

I wait for what seems like forever and taking out my phone I see that you have been in there for 30minutes and I decide that I should probably keep looking for a job myself and tear myself away. I go into a furniture store, and I think my smile gave me away.

"Hey, how are you?" The woman behind the counter asks as she finishes sanding back a piece of wood.

"Hi. Good, you?" I reply as I begin to look around the store.

"Fine. Is there something I can help you with?" She asks, coming out from behind the counter and walking over to me. I chuckle before replaying to her, knowing that I would love nothing more than to have this job, but the unlikelihood of it seems high.

"Well, you don't happen to require a new employee, do you?" I say, trying to sound as if I am joking but being very serious. The woman looks me up and down and gives me a smirk.

"Actually, yes. When can you start?" She says. I must look like a dumbfound fool as I stare plainly back at her.

"Really? You don't want to know if I know anything about making things or like, what my history is." I say, a little bit surprised.

"You're the new guy, the one with a beautiful wife. You're building that huge house along Jackson road, and from the looks of you, you are trying to build a new life along with that house," she says, making me take a step back.

"Well, yeah, that pretty much sums it up, I guess," I reply, laughing in surprise.

"Look, if you are willing to learn the trade, I can teach you everything I know, and you can just sell everything else in the meantime," she says, reaching out her hand. I smile as though I've just won the lottery and take your hand.

"You start Monday. I pay well, but I expect you to put the work in," she says, and I practically skip out of the store, and right into you.

"So, guess who is getting fucked tonight," I whisper in your ear.

"You," you reply, the smirk on your face telling me that you had been waiting here as the victor for a while.

"Really?" I laugh, looking at your beautiful face.

"Yeah. I am the new secretary. Start Monday," you explain, taking my hand and beginning to walk home with me.

"Well, good for you. I am going to get trained up to do woodwork as well as being the owner's new sales assistant. Start Monday as well," I reply.

"Well, my love. I guess we better enjoy the next few days, because we have our 9-5's secured and our new life is well underway," you say, leaning into me and kissing me deeply.

Chapter 7

It's been five months since I lost your challenge, and the house is just getting the finishing touches to it. We both like our jobs, and they have come in handy, giving us something to talk about outside of our relationship has proved essential. I used to think that I was enough to keep you entertained, thinking that if I gave you everything, that would be enough, but I was so wrong. In trying to protect you and treat you like a princess, I forgot one of the essential parts about you that you are a lot tougher than you look and that you can handle this crazy world, as long as you can balance it out with adequate downtime.

"Hey, Daddy," you call, dumping your bag by the door and walking inside to find me. I have already had a shower and am laying on the bed, more tired than usual after work today. It feels different being able to chill on a Friday afternoon than when I was working in the city. I don't thank god it's Friday anymore, but I am definitely looking forward to having you to myself for a few days.

"In here, sweetie," I call back, getting up to rest on my elbows. I wait for you to walk into the room, hearing you take off your heels and leaving them at the entrance of the room.

"Don't give me that look. I'm not there tonight, sorry," you say, as I try not to look disappointed. In truth, I love all your sides, but I was really hoping to fuck you tonight. I smile and get up, throwing a white t-shirt on and some grey track pants and wrap you up in my arms.

"Aw, does the baby need Daddy?" I coo, watching as you begin to regress. I love the way your eyes change, and your facial expressions aren't as filled with as much attitude. It's cute, and I cover your face with kisses before walking you to the bathroom.

"Not too many more baths in this house, little one," I say as I run you a bath. You have decided to crawl and have taken a little bit longer to get to the bathroom than I was expecting. I look around and find that you are nowhere to be seen, but I hear you in the bedroom.

"What are you doing in here, cheeky girl?" I ask, seeing you take out some bath toys from a box I packed a few days ago.

"I want these ones, Daddy. Please?" You ask, smiling a big toothy grin. I look at your sweet face and can't say no. I pick you up along with the bath blocks and octopus water pistol and carry you to the bathroom.

"Are you happy to play here for a little while? Daddy needs to go and get you jammies.

"Ok, Daddy," you reply, already lost in your own little world. I walk out and decide to tape up all the other boxes we have packed so you can't get into them and take out any more things. I don't know why I didn't tape them up in the first place. I think that my thoughts were that I would stuff as much stuff on top and that closing them would affect how much stuff I could add. Whatever the reason, I should have known that you would take full advantage of the situation.

I go back into the bathroom and am delighted that you have indeed washed up and are sparkly clean once again. I take you out of the bathtub and dry you off. Making a mental note that I will have to buy you some new towels when we move into our new place. I lay you down on the floor and powder you up before putting you in a big puffy diaper. You giggle and wriggle around, having not had this type on for a while.

"Hold still little one, Daddy has to put the diaper cover over this," I say, pulling up the fluffy yellow diaper cover. I pull a white singlet over your head and pull your arms through the holes, ruffling up your hair when I am finished.

"Cute little girl. You look like my own little sweet duckie," I say, running my hands over the front of your diaper. You look down and giggle as you look back up at me, your eyes sparkling.

"I'm not a duckie, Daddy," you say, making my heart instantly melt.

"Are you sure? You look like my duckie," I tease, making you giggle.

"Come on, we only have a few nights left in this house, let's have some popcorn and watch a movie, little one," I say, watching as you crawl into the living room as fast as you can go.

Moving day came sooner rather than later, and before we knew it, we were lifting furniture and directing the removalist guys where to put each thing. You looked so cute in your ripped denim overalls, pink t-shirt, and black sneakers. You wore a grey cap, and I swear the removalist guys stole a few stares when one of the front clips of your overalls broke off. I know I did, I didn't think you could look any better, but I was mistaken.

"Just put the table out the back, we will move it later, let's just get it out of the truck before it rains," you say sounding very assertive. I smirk because I haven't heard you speak like this for a long time. We stopped for lunch. I ran down to the store to get chicken and chips plus a couple of bottles of soda for everyone. The storm clouds overhead were welcomed, but they were making it very humid as they settled in.

As we took the last things out of the truck, the sky broke, and rain poured down, making me sigh with relief that nothing got wet and ruined. We thanked the removalist guys, and you paid them before we went inside, closing the door on our new and hopefully, forever home. We didn't say a word but walked to the living room which had the floor to ceiling windows looking out to the ample trees that surrounded the property. We took a moment to look around the space. The thick black carpet looked luxurious against the stark white walls. I knew that you would have some beautiful artworks in the making which we would place around those walls. The fireplace would be heaven in winter, and the high ceilings made me proud that I was able to give you such a fantastic place to call your own. The whole home was open plan, and I glanced over at the kitchen, with the black stone bench and fancy cabinets. I was surprised when you had said that we could get black appliances, but it just looks so good I'm glad it wasn't something we had to compromise on. I turn my head to look at you, and you've got that smug smile on your face.

"Pretty impressed with yourself, aren't you?" You say with a laugh.

"Yeah. I am actually," I reply, getting cuddled from you.

"I'm proud of you too, Daddy," you whisper, making my heart swell. I remember when we first got together, and you asked me what I needed after play or if there was something that I liked and I was so surprised. I hadn't thought of the type of affection I needed or liked and had sort of thought that Daddies didn't get that. That I had to be this super strong and dominant figure that never broke, but you showed me that I was wrong and that when I let myself have a softer side toward myself, that I really liked that.

"Thanks, little one," I reply, wrapping my arm around you.

"Let's get some showers in and have a little play in your nursery before bed," I suggest, making you clap your hands excitedly.

"Ok!" You exclaim and run to the bathroom.

"Oh my gosh, this is so beautiful," you say, looking around the extra-large bathroom. We knocked down a wall so that the bathroom would be almost stupidly large. It's so big that the spa bath, huge shower space, and wall-length vanity fits perfectly. You tap your feet on the floor, and I know you are feeling for the floor heating, and I chuckle.

"It's nice, hey?" I say, making you nod your head as you strip and get under the shower, the water coming out like raindrops, and you stretch your arms, unable to touch the sides of the shower.

"Yeah, this is really nice!" You exclaim, making my heart swell. You see that it wasn't the only thing to swell and raise your eyebrow.

"That impressed, are you?" You say, suddenly becoming incredibly sexual with your stare.

"You keep looking at me like that, and you'll see how impressed I am," I say, hoping that you are in the mood. I can see you are thinking about it, figuring out which space you want to be in before turning your back on me and shaking your ass on my hard cock.

"Well?" You tease, rubbing yourself from the front.

"Yeah," I reply, spreading your ass cheeks and pushing into your pussy. I slide in easily, surprised at how wet you are.

"I've been horny all day, watching your muscles flex and strain as you lifted all that stuff from the truck. I wanted you to lay me down on the couch and fuck me all day," you say, making me pound you harder. I have no interest in trying to hold back tonight and watch as your tits bounce with each thump you take from behind. I grab hold of your hair and quicken my pace, moaning as I fill you before thrusting into you a few more times before pulling out.

"And now you can make me cum," you say, almost demandingly so and I watch as you lay down on the shower floor. I lay next to you and gently rub your clit, feeling the water from the shower fall over our tired bodies as I rub you just softly, just the way you like. I can see you have the same amount of desire to cum, and I whisper that you can whenever you want. I don't want to make you wait for it tonight, and it wouldn't be fair after you let me use you. You groan and buck your hips before squeezing your thighs together tightly before flinging my hand away. I see that your leg is shaking, and I smile to myself, happy that you are mine and that I am yours.

"Do you still want to play, little one? Or are you ready for bed?" I ask after you get out of the shower, and I get you dressed. You sit at the end of the bed and think very thoughtfully, making me suppress a smirk. I let you dress yourself tonight, and you have chosen the sweetest baby pink onesie and matching bow headband.

"Can I have a little play, but I am tired, Daddy," you say as I take you in my arms and carry you to your nursery.

"Of course you can, baby girl," I say as I place you down on the floor. You crawl over to where I had set up your tea party set and watch as you get to work, making pretend cakes and pretend tea. I sit upon the custom made rocking chair I made and hummed a little tune as I watch you. It's so sweet how you line up your stuffies to make sure that everyone has a cake and some tea. Before long, you have grown tired of tea parties, and are laying on your tummy coloring in. I watch as you debate which color to put where and smirk as you start three pictures at once. I use to try and get you to finish one picture before you went onto the next, but I gave that quest up a long time ago. You yawn for the last time I'm going to let you before putting you to bed and scoop you up into my arms, not bothering to have you tidy up the room. It's been a big day, and now that you are nice and relaxed, all I can think about is getting to sleep.

"Come and cuddle with Daddy princess," I say, feeling you snuggle into my neck and hold me close. You don't protest and silently fall asleep in my arms before I have even laid you down in our new king size bed.

Chapter 8

It's about three weeks since we moved in, and our routine is simplistically beautiful. We both go to work Monday to Friday, 9-5. We go for hikes or bike rides on the weekends, do the food shop on a Thursday night, and have takeout on Mondays. We had both thoughts that having a simpler life would be nice, but it is more comfortable than I could have predicted.

"Daddy, what happened?! I got a call from Tracy saying you had an accident," you yell through the house. I'm sitting on the couch watching a movie on my phone when you finally rush into the room, gasping when you see my broken arm.

"Well, you see. I was trying to pull a plank down, and I just lost my grip, and it came down directly onto my forearm," I explain as you rush over to my side. You run your hand over my cast and look at me like I am really silly.

"It might have been a little bit too heavy," I admit making you roll your eyes.

"Serves you right for trying to show off," you reply. I love that your way of giving sympathy is almost not to give any at all.

"Yeah, well, Tracy took me to the doctors, and they patched me up real good and quick. But I have to leave this on for like seven weeks. So Daddy might need you to do a few more things around the house. Can you do that for me, sweetheart?" I ask. You nod your head and snuggle into my side, making me smile.

"Let's watch this together," you suggest, and I turn the movie back on.

"Daddy, I want to get in my jammies," you say, looking up at me. Usually, I would have you bathed by now, but the pain killers I was given by the doctor have made me unusually tired. I yawn and stretch my good arm, before getting up and holding out my hand to you. You take it happily and stand up, walking with me to the bathroom.

"You know the drill, little lady," I say, sitting by the bath and running it for you. You turn on some music before you jump in, splashing in the bubble bath and washing away the stress from the day. I see that you have had enough and pull the plug on your bath, making you begin to rush to get out, you like to get out of the bath before the water is completely gone.

"Can you dry yourself tonight, little one?" I ask, handing you the towel.

"Such a good girl," I say as you nod your head, yes, and I walk into your nursery to find what I want you to wear tonight. We haven't got curtains on the windows yet, but I kind of figured that being surrounded by forest, the chances of someone seeing us is really low.
You crawl into the nursery and go straight over to your paci you left in your cot and begin sucking it. I tap the changing mat on the floor, and you come over to me, laying on your back expectantly.

"I need you to hold it here, sweetie," I say as

I begin to fasten the diaper to you. You giggle as you watch me struggle. Not only did I break my hand, but I also broke my writing hand. Finally, I have you diapered, and I take out your cloud onesie and let you help do up the clips at the front.

"Good girl," I say, letting you sit in my lap. I suddenly look up as I heard something coming from the door but relaxed when I guessed it was just an animal or branch from a tree falling. It has taken a bit of getting used to having these new sounds around.

"Daddy, what's for dinner?" I hear you ask, and I am so grateful that it is a takeout night. If I am honest, I would have let you have takeout tonight regardless of what day it was, and I set you up in front of the television before I begin to walk out the door. As I open it, I stop dead in my tracks and feel my stomach lurch. That was no animal I heard making the noise outside. That was my boss. On the front stoop, there is a lasagne with a note saying, *Get it while it's hot, Tracy.* I wonder how much she has seen, I wonder what she thinks of me, some people don't get it and think it's sick or a dangerous kink, but it's not. I hate kids, and I just love having my partner need me like a Daddy. I find it a nicer way of being a Dom, but like anything, it's not for everyone. What if she tells everyone in town, what if I get fired or worse, what if they make our life here miserable?! I don't tell you any of this and simply continue out to pick up burgers and fries.

I am not looking forward to going back to work today as I step foot through the door, causing the bell to ring.

"Hey," Tracy says as if everything is fine. I look at her and can see on her face that she saw something last night.

"Hi," I reply, trying not to be sick with anxiety.

We spend the whole day trying to act like everything is normal, and at 3 pm, when the store goes quiet, I look at her and can't keep avoiding this situation any longer.

"What I am assuming you saw last night, let me explain it to you, please," I say, trying to stay calm. I never thought I would be having this conversation with someone, let alone my boss.

"What I saw? How you're a Daddy, and your wife is your little one? That's what you are meaning?" She replies, a smirk on her face. I must have looked shocked because she rolls her eyes at me before speaking again.

"Dude, chill. Why do you think I hired you? I could tell you, and I had stuff in common the moment I looked at you. We Doms have that whole, and we run the world thing going. It's an easy thing to read," Tracy explained, making me shake my head.

"Woah," is all I could say, and I sat down behind the counter.

"So, all this time?" I asked, looking at her out of the corner of my eye. She just nodded her head slowly and came behind the counter as well.

"I've lived here most of my life, so I can say with 100% certainty that no one will be able to tell the dynamic you guys have. That's why I always take a month off and go to the city. Because it is near impossible to explore being a caregiver out here," she continued making me laugh.

"Yeah, I kind of figured that. I'm shocked, and I didn't see this coming," I said honestly, making her laugh and disappear out the back.

"Wait," I called when the idea struck me. I followed her out the back and into the woodshed, the last time I was here I broke my arm, so I was cautious about what I was doing.

"Why don't I have a party? That way, you won't have to wait until the holidays to have a bit of fun. I know some great people, and the house is big enough that everyone could stay over. We could make a weekend of it if you're interested?" I offered, hoping that she would agree.

"Keep talking like that, and you'll be looking at a raise," Tracy joked before looking very serious.

"I would really love that, Craig," she added, making me proud that I had made my first and probably the only friend in the community in this small little town.

"Baby girl, Daddy has a treat for you," I call out into the house the moment I am home. I went to the toy store as well as the frozen yogurt store and picked you up a few things. I am grateful that the frozen yogurt shop is close to our house and that it is a cool day because I would have hated if it had melted too much. I hear your giggles and creep closer to where I can listen to you telling your stuffies to be quiet.

"Where could my little one be? Oh well, if I can't find her, I guess I just have to eat this giant frozen yogurt all by myself," I tease and wait for you to pop your head out of wherever you are.

"Daddy!" You exclaim and jump up from behind the couch, running over to me.

"Hey, there little cutie. We are celebrating!" I say, taking down a bottle of whiskey and managing to pour myself a drink.

"What are we celebrating?" You ask, sitting

up at the kitchen bench. I'm not sure how you've managed, but you have yogurt all over your face already, and I try not to laugh at how funny you look.

"Ok, so, Tracy, my boss. She's a Mommy," I say. I am aware of how happy I sound but soon frown at you when you do not match my enthusiasm.

"Ok?" You question.

"So?" You add.

"So?! So now we can have a play party, and we have someone in the kink to like, mesh with!" I say, regaining my excitement. At this point, you just laugh and shake your head.

"Ok," you say, shrugging your shoulders. Clearly, I have missed something here because I thought you would be excited to have a little bit of community around.

"So, you aren't interested in having a party?" I ask, coming to sit next to you.

"Oh no, I am," you reply, making me even more confused.

"Then why don't you seem excited or at least interested?" I say, trying to get to the real reason for your withdrawal of energy. You put your yogurt down and look me dead in the eye.

"She's really beautiful. Like in an edgy, sexy woodland woman way. What if you fall for her and want her to be my Mommy? I don't want a Mommy," you say, finally making everything make sense. I scoop you into my arms and kiss your forehead.

"There is no way I am letting her be your Mommy, little girl. You are Daddy's, and only his and I am not sharing you at all, ever, ok?" I say, trying to reassure you.

"Is that for me?" You say, pointing to the toy bag on the floor. I laugh and nod, picking the bag up and placing it on the bench.

"I am so grumpy that you know me so well!" You say, trying to keep sounding guarded and angry. I just chuckle as you pull out the unicorn with the purple wings you saw last week and squeal.

"Daddy!" You say, holding onto it tightly and rocking back and forth.

"See, princess. It's just like in the old house where we both had friends in the scene. Nothing ever happened that we both didn't want, and it'll be the same here. Plus, I don't think she's hot, I prefer my girls all cute and giggly," I say tickling you and making you run away to the safety of your pillow fort.

Chapter 9

The noise could be heard from outside, that's generally what happens when I throw a party. I don't like to do things in halves, so when I host, I host! While I have a strict no-alcohol rule, the music and the vibe of the party creates for a lot of laughter and fun. The backyard was the mutual area, and I had strung up some fairy lights to give it a relaxed and calming atmosphere. There was a few tapas platers, and a lot of the people started off out there. Most of the people that had arrived were people we had known back in the city, so it was great to catch up and show them around the house and property. You loved it too, showing off your room to the delight and mild jealousy of the other littles. Each room of our house had people staying in them for the weekend; however, for the duration of the party, the rooms would be used for giving aftercare or for sexual play. I had gone over the rules, making sure everyone was on the same page. A few of my friends had bought their new little, Mommy or Daddy, and I made sure that they knew the score before our fun began. You had taken great care in setting up your nursery and the media room for the other littles to color or play in.

"Hey, I'm so glad you could make it," I say, seeing Tracy walk through the door. She smiles and hands me her coat, and I hang it up before turning back to her.

"Wow, it's just as nice on the inside as the outside," she says, making me smile.

"Let me introduce you to Billie," I say, leading her into your nursery.

"Hey, sweet girl. Do you remember Tracy from Daddy's work," I say. You took forever to choose an outfit tonight. It's not that you are the crazy jealous type, but I can understand why you feel vulnerable and insecure sometimes.

"Hi Tracy," you say, and she gets down to your level and looks you in the eye, amused when you don't look away.

"That's a really pretty dress you've got on Billie," she says, making you reluctantly smile.

"Thank you," you say, and I realize I've been holding my breath.

"Don't worry sweetie, I don't want your Daddy," Tracy whispers to you and reaches out and strokes your cheek before winking at you.

"I like her," you say loudly before going back to coloring in with your friends.

"How did you know?" I ask Tracy as we walk out onto the back porch and get a soda.

"She might be your little, but she's still a woman," Tracy replies, making me laugh. I must admit, sometimes I do forget that you're my 29-year-old sexy wife and, of course, you would have normal adult feelings.

We chat about work, watch the littles play, and Tracy catches the eye of a little boy who you have been friends with for years.

"Hi handsome, what are you doing?" She says, coming to sit next to me and you on the couch. Hamish, the man she is referring to, is a personal trainer from the city who has always had a hard time keeping a Mommy. He is really clingy, something that everyone says they find cute until it gets annoying. You're sitting on my lap, and I am stroking your hair as I chat to another Daddy about how nice life is out here.

"Hey," Hamish quietly says, he is busy stacking very thin blocks into a tower, and I can tell you are fighting the urge to kick his tower over. You can be a little monster like that sometimes.

"Can I play?" Tracy asks, making Hamish look up at her with his usual puppy dog eyes full of devotion. He just nods, and I can feel you fidgeting.

"No," I say, looking you dead in the eye, I can tell you are about to get up to mischief.

"You're really good at that," Tracy says, and then almost on cue, your foot goes out and knocks over the meter-high tower over, making Hamish almost cry. He looks up at you, and you snicker, making my conversation come to a halt.

"It's ok, honey, and I can help you make a

new tower if you'd like?" Tracy says, taking Hamish's hand and looking at him lovingly. He bites his bottom lip and wipes away a tear that has escaped his eye.

"Do you want a cuddle little prince?" Tracy says, Hamish just nods.

"You need to say sorry to Hamish for knocking his tower over. That was really mean and rude," I say to you. You look at me as though you thought you had gotten away with being a brat and shake your head at me. Usually, I would have given you some warning, but I flipped you over and spanked your ass so fast that you couldn't stop it from happening.

"Daddy!" You whinge, only adding to my annoyance.

"Count," I bark, watching as Hamish crawled into Tracy's lap, and she began to rock him in her arms.

"One," you whimper. I'm glad it's caught you off guard, and I'm glad that you can feel it. I hate bratty girls, and I also hate my baby being mean on purpose.

"Two, three, four, five," you continue to pant. I stop at five, knowing that I have put more into these spanks that I usually would have. I run my hand over your ass and pull your head back up to force you to look at me.

"I said, you need to say sorry to Hamish for being mean and rude, kicking his tower over," I growl, hoping that you take the hint. You look at me for a moment and then turn to face Hamish and Tracy.

"Sorry I knocked your tower over, Hamish," you say loudly, knowing that a bad apology will just get you more spanks on your already sore bottom. Hamish just nods his head and says thank you softly before snuggling into Tracy, and I pick you up and carry you into our bedroom.

"You were really naughty tonight, young lady," I say, laying you down on the bed. You wriggle around, and I can tell that you are going to take a long time to settle. I go back to the door and lock it. I don't want anyone disturbing us. I watch as you give me a cheeky smirk and roll my eyes.

"Do you really think you are going to get what you want, behaving like a brat?" I ask as you giggle and roll over, wiggling your ass in the air.

The night proceeded with Tracey and Hamish leaving together, and your ass being turned bright red. I smiled as I watched you fall asleep in my arms, and as I drifted off to sleep, I thought about how lucky I was that this was my life and how precious you looked falling asleep in Daddy's arms.

Who is Tina Moore?

Tina Moore has enjoyed the lifestyle of a Mommy Domme for several years. She began exploring kink and BDSM in her youth and found her love of being a strict Mommy Domme in early 2000. Tina Moore is now an author of many MDLG, DDLG and ABDL themed novels.

Follow her on:

Author Page on Amazon

Instagram @tinamoore.kdp

If you enjoyed this book, it would be much appreciated if you leave **a review**.